AF674208

Limericks on E.N.T. Disorders

Copyright ©2021. Dr. Rajendra Shantaram Balge All rights reserved.

The characters and events portrayed in this book are fictitious. Any similarity to real persons, living or dead, is coincidental and not intended by the author.

No part of this book may be reproduced, or stored in a retrieval system, or transmitted in any form or by any means, electronic, mechanical, photocopying, recording, or otherwise, without express written permission of the author.

The information provided in this book is designed to provide helpful information on the subjects discussed. This book is not meant to be used, nor should it be used, to diagnose or treat any medical condition. For diagnosis or treatment of any medical problem, consult your doctor. The author is not responsible for any specific health or allergy needs that may require medical supervision and is not liable for any damages or negative consequences from any treatment, action, application or preparation, to any person reading or following the information in this book.

ISBN: 978-93-5445-008-2

Questions / Queries / Feedback?

Email: book@hadnow.com

Cover Concept & Design by:

Preethi & Prakash Balge
India

In memory of my mother, Snehalatha and my father Shantaram.

Always remember........

We must help nature....

And let nature help us.

About the author

Dr. Rajendra S Balge joined the E.N.T. Department of B. J. Medical College, Ahmedabad after M.B.B.S. He did his D.L.O. and M. S. (E.N.T.) and joined his father, Dr. Shantaram Shrinivas Balge in private practice.

Dr. S. S. Balge was the professor and Head of Department of E. N. T. in B. J. Medical College.

Rajendra has a brother Manohar, who is also an E. N. T. Specialist and a sister Ashoka.

Acknowledgement

The illustrations used in this book are from freepik.com under Premium subscription. I thank the authors / creators on freepik.com for providing the illustrations.

The cover image is from pixabay.com. I thank the author on pixabay.com for providing the image.

The illustrations & diagrams used in the book are for representational purpose only.

The fonts used in the print edition are EB Garamond and Berkshire Swash (also used on the cover and back). I thank the authors of the fonts.

Contents

Please read this book slowly and enjoy.

Do not reveal the end to anyone, girl or boy.

If you like the book, then tell someone you like.

If you do not like, then tell someone you dislike.

Who knows, you may start liking the person you dislike.

Introduction

Basically I am a very lazy person. What better activity could such a person have than reading. Hence it became my hobby. I used to appreciate that the writer has taken pains to think and write so that we can have something to read. I never thought that one day I would be writing something myself.

Although I have written some small articles, poetry in the past usually it was limited to a couple of pages and that was before I started medical practice.

After that I was busy in my routine work to even think of writing.

Now that I have almost retired, my son Prakash often tells me to write something. After a lot of prodding, I decided to write. I thought why not write something about the subject I know i.e ear, nose, throat and at the same time satisfy my wish to write poetry

During my practice, I found that prevention is always better than cure and at times prevention was the only cure and everyone who comes to me with a problem or symptom does not necessarily have any disease. We can prevent only if we have basic knowledge of the disease. I hope after going through this, you will find something useful which is helpful in prevention of some of the ENT disorders.

I also found that the patients want to know something about the problem they have, its cause. I would therefore like to write some things which would help understand the problem. Sometimes it becomes difficult for the doctor to explain each and every aspect. Usually the doctor would write the treatment to be taken by the patient, and that's it. For explanation and understanding, I may give examples, which may not be scientifically 100% similar, but they are given so that the problem can be understood easily.

Also nowadays, if we want to know something about anything, we search the net. So there's no point in writing those things here.

So, I am just sharing with you the names of the disorders which I have come across frequently during my practice in the form of Limericks and story.

To satisfy my wish to write poetry, I thought of writing a story in limerick form, which was the one I liked the most when I studied in school. I did not like poetry, but I still remember, I enjoyed reading a portion of Edward Lear's 'Book of Nonsense', which we had to study. It went something like this;

"The owl and the pussycat went to sea

In a beautiful pea green boat

They took some honey

And plenty of money

Wrapped in a five pound note"

To make it a bit interesting, there is a plot in my story and naturally it has got to do with ENT problems.

I have written some explanations in prose form, so that things are somewhat clearer for the reader.

At the end, there is a collection of a few things I wrote before I became busy with my practice.

I wish to thank my father for the knowledge he imparted and my mother for the wisdom. I wish to thank my wife, Chandrika, for the inspiration she gave. I wish to thank Prakash, my son and Preethi my daughter in law, without whose efforts, this would not have seen the light of the day.

If you like what I have written, tell someone you like,

if not tell someone you dislike.

If you love a person, gift this.

Enjoy!

On a hot and sultry afternoon

We were waiting for the monsoon

My son told me

To write poetry

So I am writing this from June

I am a doctor by profession

And writing is not my passion

But I thought

Why should I not

Write something in a simple fashion

I am a specialist in ENT

It is called otorhinolaryngology

If I am not wrong

As we go along

You'll know something about the specialty

Before going to the clinic I read the news,
mostly the headline and some views.

After walking,

And some resting,

I do not forget to have my fruit juice.

Returning from the clinic, when I come home

I read in detail, when I am alone

The editorial page

And at my age

This is better than going out and roam

Newspapers tell us all about the universe

Economy going from bad to worse

It also shows us

Without any fuss

How to save money in our purse

Newspaper these days are full of ads

Cartoon corner enjoyed by girls and lads

Big catastrophies

And bigger controversies

You know about the latest fashion fads

Politics, religion, sports, you name it
You know about everything a little bit
Sudoku, horoscope
Like a kaleidoscope
Its the best thing to have when you sit

Most of the news is very general
And almost all may be dull
Once in a while
You get to smile
Especially when you have solved a puzzle

In our town there was a robbery

In the home of a person known to me

Though no one was hurt

In spite of some effort

The robber managed to flee

The Police Inspector who handled the case

Met me today, face to face

He wished he knew

Or had a cue

To pinpoint the robber of this place

The Family

Badam
Eldest Son
Kesar
Wife of Kaju
Kaju
Akhrot
Second Son
Pista
Daughter
Kishmish
Sister
Badam
Eldest Son
Dalchini
Wife of Badam
Sasam
Badam & Dalchini's Son
Kaju's Family
Methi
Pista and Clove's Daughter
Pista
Daughter
Clove
Husband of Pista
Akhrot
Second Son
Elaichi
Wife of Akhrot
Kothmir
Akhrot and Elaichi's Son
Pudina
Akhrot and Elaichi's Daughter

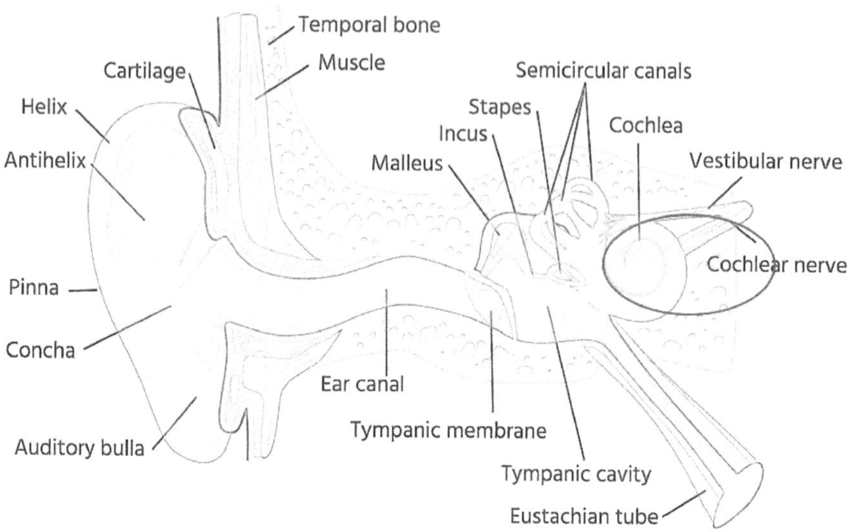

Presbyacusis - old age (senile) deafness

Apart from impaired hearing there is loss of discrimination and hence it is difficult to differentiate similar sounding words.

Kaju was a rich and old man

Who lived in a mansion with his clan

He could hardly hear

When spoken from near

When the talk is of "fan" he'll feel it is "pan"

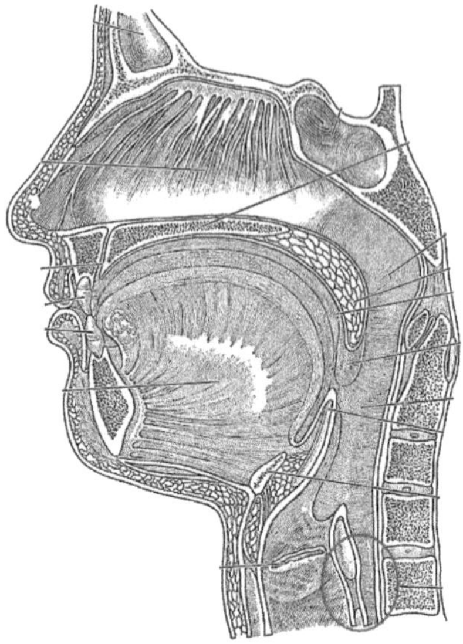

Plummer Vinson Syndrome (Peterson-Brown Kelly Syndrome)

It usually affects females above forty. They have iron deficiency – anaemia and difficulty in swallowing. They have stomatitis glossitis and koilonychia (spoon shaped) nails. If not treated its a precancerous condition. For prevention, check haemoglobin level. If its low, find the cause and treat it.

He was married to a lady named Kesar

She died sometime back of cancer

She had anaemia

And koilonychia

Now Kaju was all alone without her

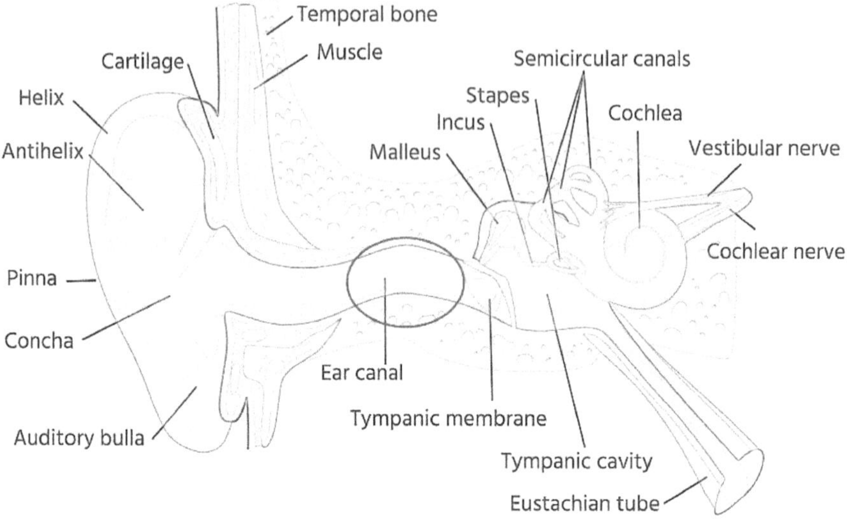

Wax

Wax is the natural secretion of the ear canal and need not be removed. However, if it has accumulated along with keratin (dead layer of the skin) giving pain, impaired hearing, itching etc. it should be removed. In such cases, do not use ear buds inside the canal as it will push the matter deeper in the canal giving more discomfort.

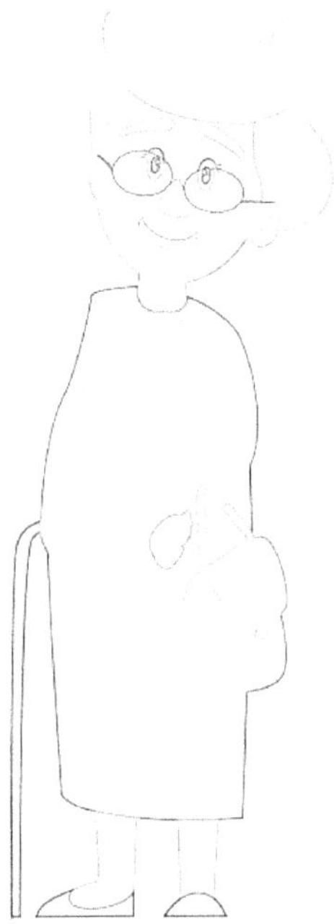

Kishmish was Kaju's only sister

She was their regular visitor

Her ears had wax

And heels had cracks

She was married to a commoner

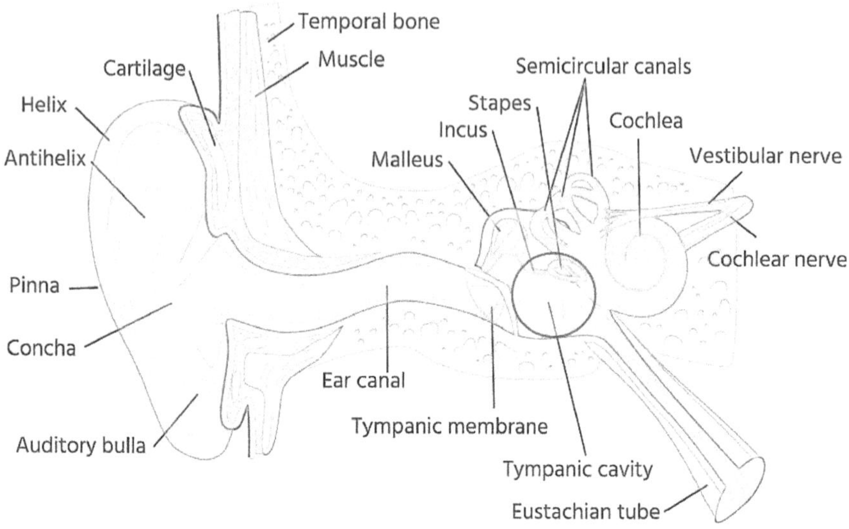

Secretory Otitis Media

Secretory Otitis Media or serous OM is a condition where fluid gets accumulated in the middle due to obstruction of a tube connecting the ear and the nasopharynx. Flying may aggravate the condition especially during descent of the flight. Symptoms are less on yawning or swallowing movements. Those who are prone to this should keep something in the mouth and swallow saliva off and on, especially during descent.

Badam is the name of his eldest son

Secretory otitis was his main concern

Whenever he'll fly

He'll wonder why

His ears were blocked without any reason

NOSE ANATOMY

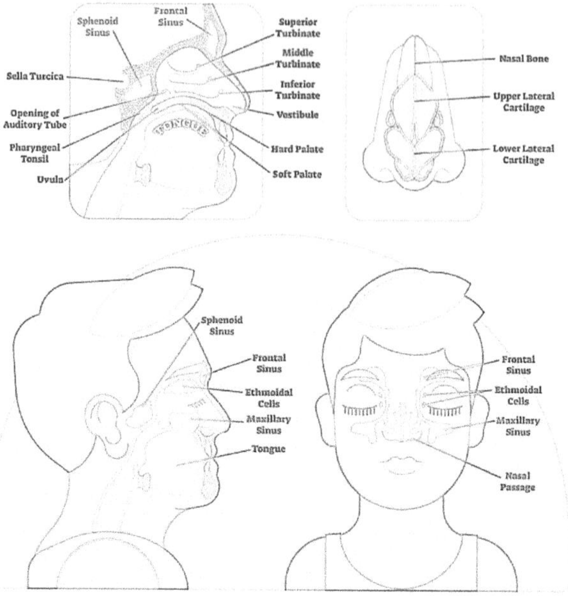

Nasal Polypi

Nasal Polypi produce nasal obstruction and discharge from the nose. If allergic in nature, there is also sneezing.

Dalchini, his wife had nasal polypi

When he went out she said bye, bye

Her nasal obstruction

Gave her some tension

She would feel that she is going to die

Snoring

Snoring, as we all know is a problem for others than the person who snores and is not disturbed. In some cases, however, there is what is known as sleep apnea, when a person stops breathing for ten seconds or more repeatedly.

Akrot was the second and always snoring

Round as a walnut and quite boring

Hence his wife was mad

But she was so glad

When he went out of town touring

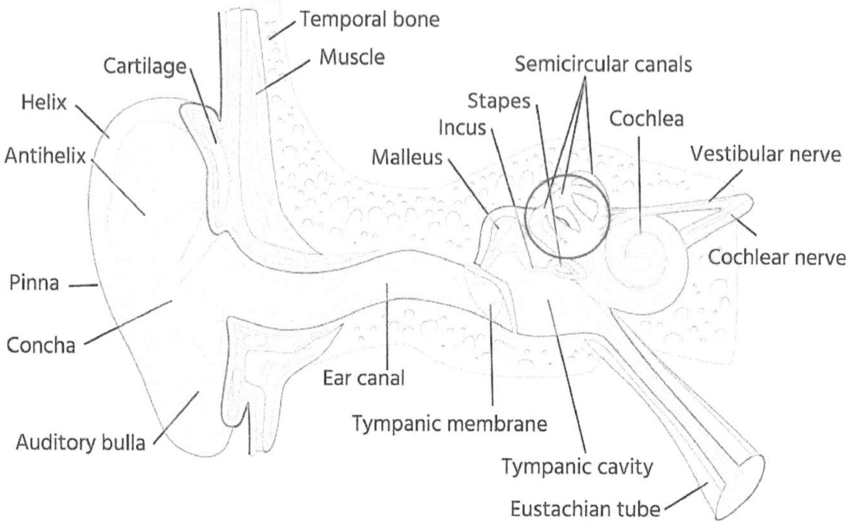

Meniere's Syndrome

Meniere's Syndrome or disease named after a French physician who described it. The patient has giddiness, deafness and tinnitus – i.e. (noises heard in the ears or head without external stimulus). There may be nausea or vomiting, headache and anxiety.

His wife Elaichi had Meniere's

With impaired hearing she had tinnitus

She felt she would fall

When she danced like a doll

And then she would almost be in tears

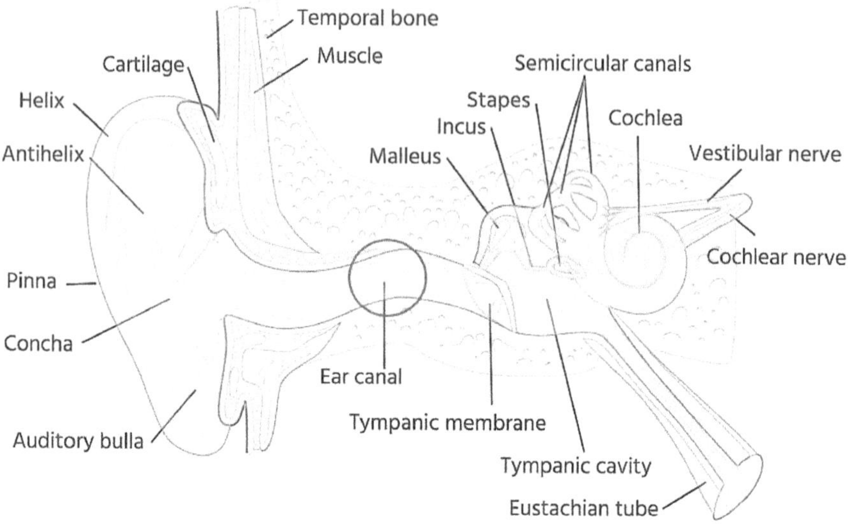

Otitis Externa

In otitis externa, there is inflammation in the external ear due to water entering the ear or due to scratching. In diabetes it is usually severe, the pain is also unbearable and if not treated, there are complications. Otomycosis is fungal infection due to water entering the ear, prolonged use of antibiotic or steroid ear drops.

Pista was the name of their dear sis

She had otitis externa and otomycosis

To remain trim

She visited a gym

And swimming was a habit she would not miss

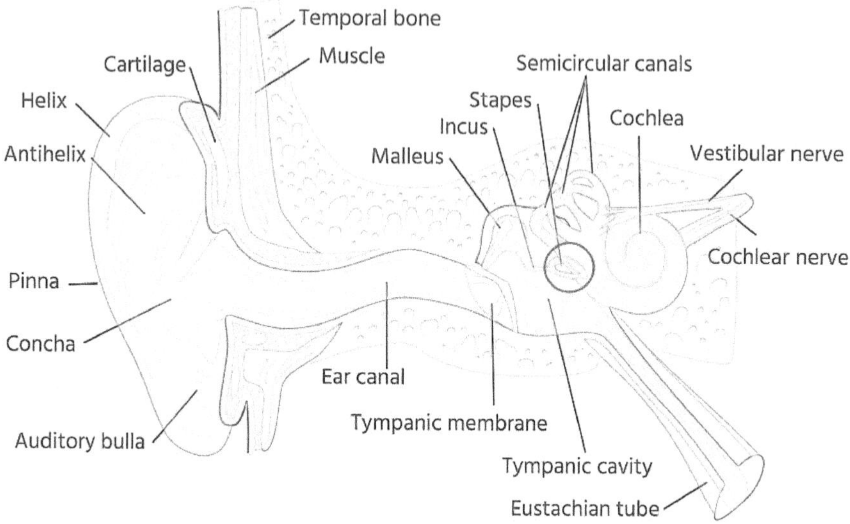

Otosclerosis

Otosclerosis is due to fixation of stapes to the oval window. There is conducive deafness in spite of normal drum and patent Eustachian tube. Such a person hears better in noisy surroundings (Paracusis Willisi). Tinnitus or noise in the ear may also be present.

Pista's spouse Clove had otosclerosis

He felt at times, he was hearing a hiss

One thing was queer

That he could hear

Better in noisy places, due to paracusis

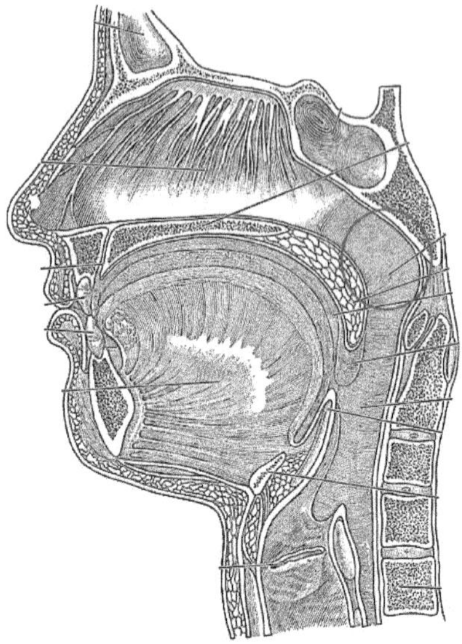

Naso pharyngeal angiofibroma

Naso pharyngeal angiofibroma is a vascular (non-malignant) benign tumour in the nasopharynx in male adolescents. There is blocking of nose and bleeding from the nose at times. Voice is changed because of blocked nose. It has to be excised taking adequate precaution due to severe bleeding problems.

Sasam, Badam's son had Angio fibroma

He was confused between Osama & Obama

Once when he was reading

He had nasal bleeding

He went out running saying mamma o' mamma

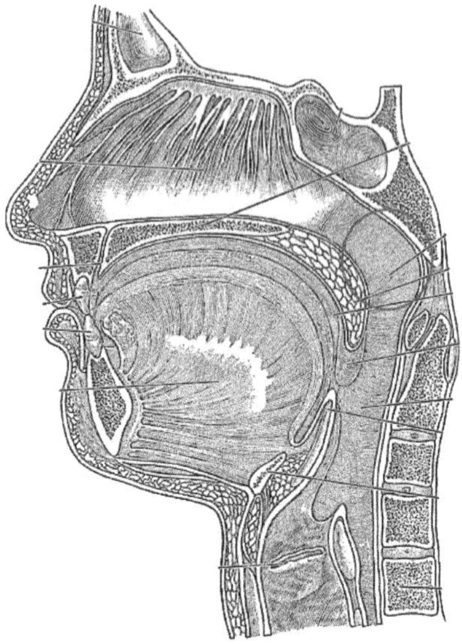

Adenoids

Adenoids are lymphoid tissues in the naso pharynx which when enlarged give nasal obstruction. Hence the child keeps the mouth open. Sometimes it leads to obstruction of the Eustachian tube leading to middle ear problems.

Methi, Clove's child was fond of stensils

She was often seen sharpening her pencils

when told to run

She kept her mouth open

As she had enlarged adenoids and tonsils

Foreign bodies

Foreign bodies are usually inserted by children. Sometimes scented objects may enter accidentally while trying to smell. Sometimes children do not tell anyone out of fear or ignorance. If there is unilateral discharge/ bleeds from the nostrils, always look for a foreign body.

Akrot & Elaichi were parents of two children

Pudina the daughter and Kothmir the son

The son would stuff his nose

With petals of rose

But removing the foreign bodies was no fun

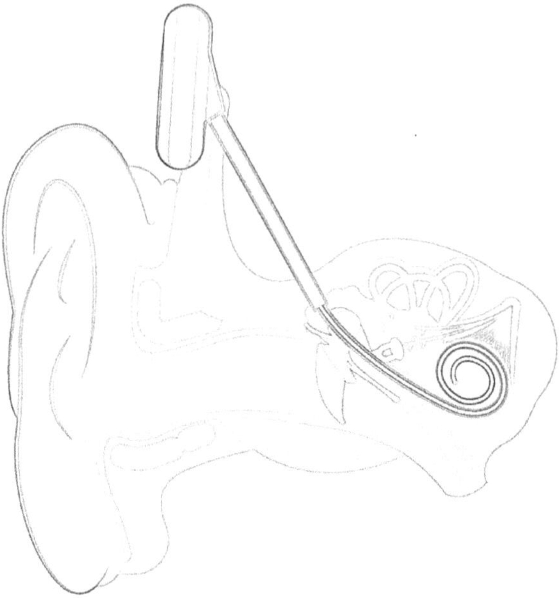

Cochlear implant

In spite of the fact that the speech centre and speech organs are normal, a child may not speak because of severe loss of hearing before a child learns to speak. Hearing aid and speech therapy is helpful. Cochlear implants may be considered when there is damage in the cochlea with such severe deafness that even a hearing aid does not help.

Pudina the daughter was born deaf

She looked somewhat like Katrina Kaif

She loved to dance

And used to glance

At the photos of her hero named Saif

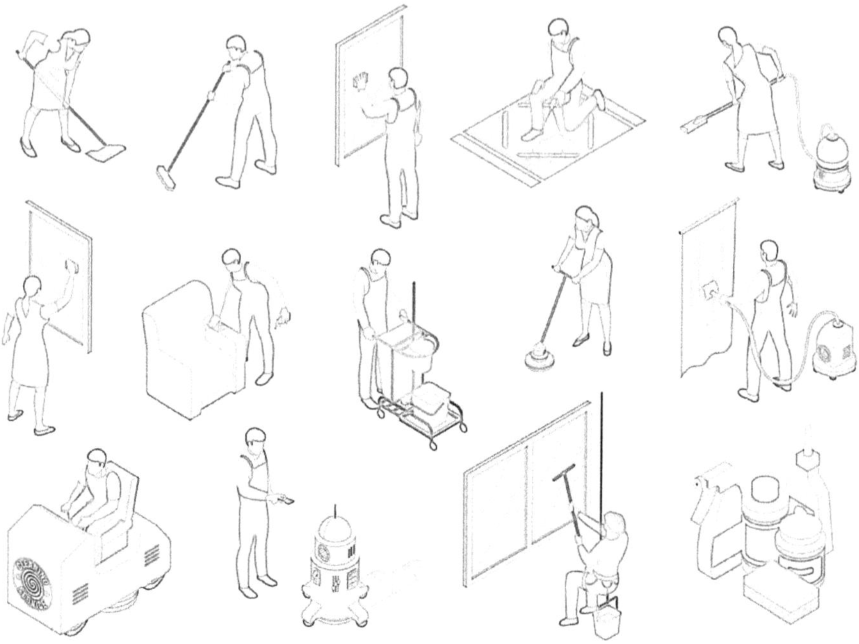

Staff Working

Staff

Mango – The butler – Vocal nodules

Litchi(Mango's wife) – Anosmia

Suran – The Gardener – Chronic Otitis Media & Sinusitis

Kakdi(Suran's Wife) – Fractured nasal bone

Kaddu – Driver of Badam – Submucous fibrosis & Stomatitis

Bhindi(Kaddu's wife) – Traumatic perforation of the ear drum

Aloo – Akrot's driver – Acoustic neuroma

Gobhi(Aloo's wife & Elaichi's maid) – Facial palsy

Matar – Housekeeper – Cancer larynx

Mooli(Matar's wife) – GERD

Fanas – Pista's driver – MunchHausen's Syndrome

Dudhi(Fanas's Wife) - Coryza

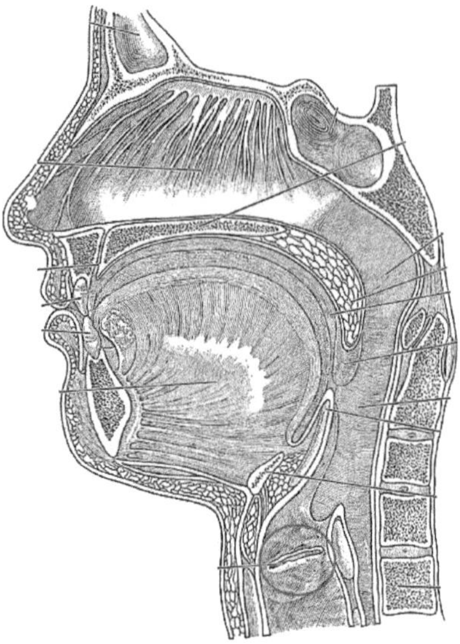

Hoarse Voice

A hoarse voice is produced due to misuse or over use of voice. If it persists for more than a couple of weeks laryngeal examination is required to determine the exact cause especially to rule out malignancy, chronic infection, paralysis etc.

Mango was the butler with a hoarse voice

He would shout at all the girls & boys

To get the work done

And it was no fun

But he would walk about with a certain poise

Anosmia

Anosmia means loss of sense of smell. It may be due to obstruction in the nasal cavity due to polypi or neoplasms or neurological either traumatic or intracranial lesions. Whenever there is anosmia, the flavour of food is not perceived. It may also be a symptom of Covid-19

Litchi, his wife had a distinct look

Inspite of anosmia, she was a great cook

Everyone loved her food

And it was so good

Although she never ever read a cookbook

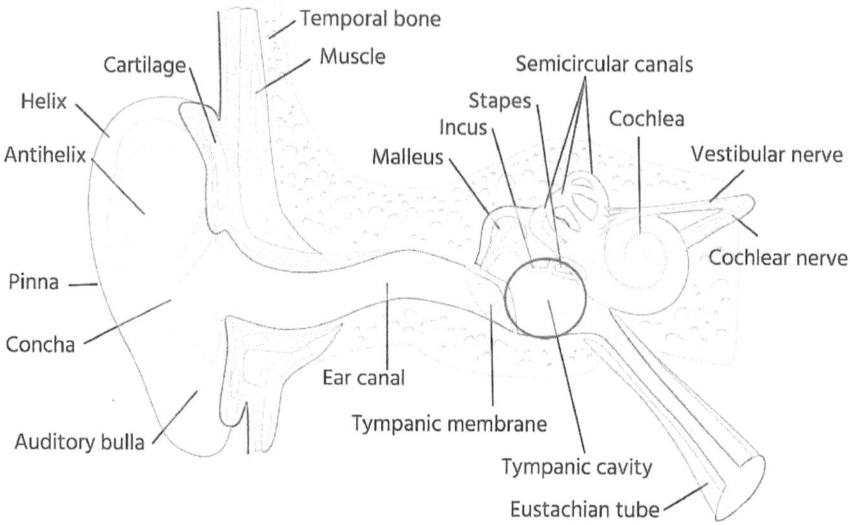

Chronic otitis media

Chronic otitis media is infection of the middle ear. If there is a central perforation*, it is not dangerous. However, if there is cholesteatoma where there is marginal or attic perforation, then there is a likelihood of life threatening complications.

* *(Respiratory tract infection including sinusitis is a predisposing factor)*

Sinusitis gives rise to pain, nasal discharge and blocking of nose. There may be dry cough due to post nasal discharge. Malaise headache are the general symptoms. It may be acute or chronic. In acute cases the symptoms may be accompanied by fever too.

Now lets look at all the other staff

Suran the gardener would never laugh

His chronic otitis

And his sinusitis

Was the cause of worry for his better half

Fracture of nasal bones

Fracture of nasal bones occurs due to direct injury on the nose or head injury accompanied by nasal fracture. There is swelling around the nose, bleeding from nose and blocking of nose. If there is bleeding between the layers of nasal septum, there may be septal haematoma. It is best to reduce the fracture before swelling of soft tissue develops.

In children, when there is injury on the nose, there is likelihood of blood accumulation between the septum and there is swelling and nasal obstruction. That has to be drained as early as possible, otherwise, cartilage of the nose gets eroded and the shape of the nose gets altered.

Kakdi was the name of Suran's spouse

Her main job was that of cleaning the house

Once she injured her nose

Which was as red as a rose

It happened when she was chasing a mouse

Stomatitis

Stomatitis is inflammation in the oral cavity. In recurrent ulcerative stomatitis there is pain. The exact cause is not known but may be due to irritants or toxins or auto immune factors.

In oral submucous fibrosis, there is deposit of fibrous tissues under the mucosa in the oral cavity. Hence there is difficulty in opening the mouth. It may be a collagen disorder. It occurs mainly in the Indian subcontinent, usually due to eating "pan masala" - chewing betel nut/leaf with tobacco.

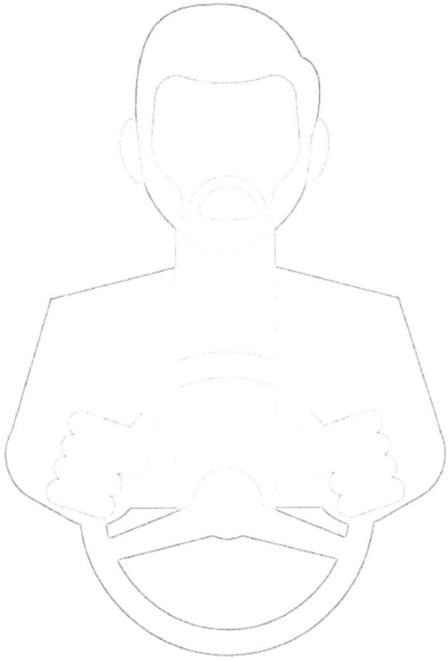

Kaddu was Badam & Dalchini's driver

He was a constant "pan masala" chewer

He had stomatitis

And submucous fibrosis

His mouth could hardly open a finger

Traumatic perforation of the tympanic membrane (ear drum)

Traumatic perforation of the tympanic membrane (ear drum) occurs usually due to slapping on the ear, sometimes when trying to clean the ear or while removing foreign bodies. It may also occur due to blasts or cracker explosion nearby. It is very important to remember that in such cases, ear drops should not be put. Naturally, water too should not enter till the perforation heals which is around 8 weeks. Those which do not heal may require surgery.

Bhindi, Kaddu's wife was fond of curry

Her job was to clean the cutlery

She injured her ear

And could not hear

When she tried to prevent burglary

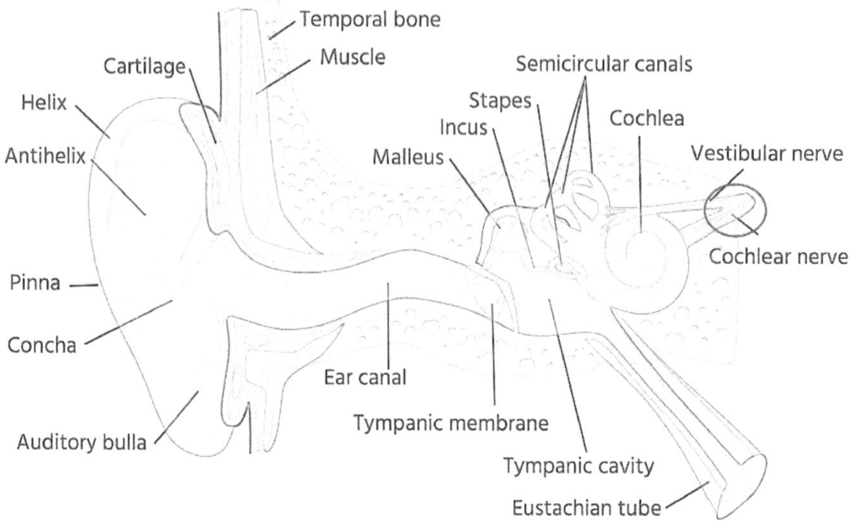

Acoustic Neuroma

Acoustic Neuroma is a slow growing tumour of the cover of the auditory nerve giving rise to gradually increasing sensorineural hearing loss and tinnitus. Excessive use of mobile phone is one of the reasons which may be responsible, although, there is some doubt.

Aloo was the driver and Akrot was his boss

He used to talk a lot on his mobile without a pause

Sometimes he would wonder

And at times he would ponder

Why was it that he had a hearing loss

Bells Palsy (Facial Palsy)

Bells Palsy (Facial Palsy) usually occurs after exposure to cold. The eyelid on the affected side cannot be closed and the angle of the mouth deviates towards the normal side and dribbling of saliva. Most of the cases recover.

Gobhi, Elaichi's maid had facial palsy

She loved to learn new words, you see

Once sitting on a bench

She heard some French

And picked up the words "Tres Bien Merci"

Cancer of the larynx

Cancer of the larynx usually occurs in smokers. If it is restricted to the vocal cord and diagnosed early it can be treated by radiotherapy with excellent long-term results. However, if there is fixation of the vocal cords or there is residual recurrence of growth after radiotherapy, removal of larynx (laryngectomy) is done. Hence a tracheostomy (hole in the trachea) is performed for breathing air.

Matar was the general housekeeper

He was an almost constant smoker

He had laryngectomy

And also tracheostomy

When he was treated for laryngeal cancer

GERD or Gastro Oesophageal Reflex Disease

GERD or Gastro Oesophageal Reflex Disease is quite common. Patients complain of eructation, burning in the throat, hoarseness of voice etc. The acid from the stomach gets regurgitated upwards. It is advisable not to have heavy meals at night or keep a gap of at least 3-4 hours before going to bed, after having a good meal at night.

Mooli, Matar's wife had GERD

She was wondering what it was, you see

She was happy to learn

That it was heartburn

Now she controls herself when she drinks tea

M. H (Munchhausen's) Syndrome

M. H (Munchhausen's) Syndrome is a condition when patient feels he has some or the other disease and takes unnecessary treatment and sometimes undergoes unnecessary surgeries too.

Fanas, Pista's driver was hardly at home
Whenever possible he would go out & roam
Imagining he had diseases
He'll undergo surgeries
He had what's called Munchausen's syndrome

Coryza or common cold

Coryza or common cold is well known. They say if you treat a cold, it lasts a week. If you do not, it lasts for seven days. It is caused by viruses. Treatment is usually symptomatic and hot fluids, steam inhalation helps. Prevention is by avoiding direct contact with the person infected, cleaning hands often, not touching the nose and avoid being around an affected person, who is sneezing or coughing.

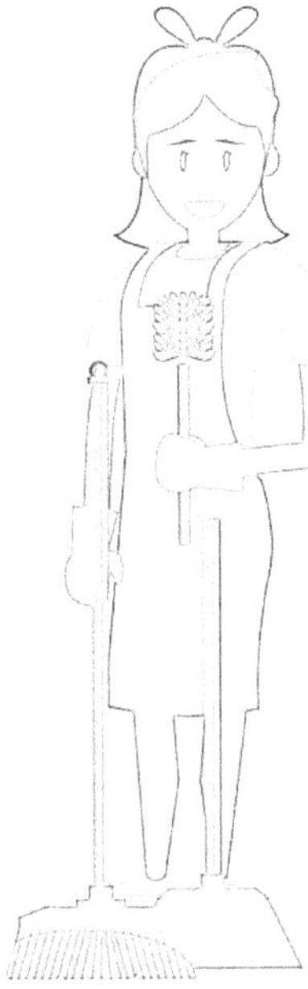

Dudhi, Fanas's wife had a heart of gold

She always thought she was very bold

Once she was diagnosed

Coryza and she dozed

After taking pills for her common cold

This is a story of a very rich man who had willed his property equally among his children and staff members. He was hard of hearing. Then one day, he started using a hearing aid and did not tell anyone. He started hearing what everyone said about him. They were not aware of his use of hearing aid. He found that everyone was interested in his money. So he decided to change his will and called a lawyer. As you have seen, all members of the family and staff have some ENT disorder. One person sent a thief to steal the new will. WHO COULD IT BE?! Only one person could know that the old man was talking to the lawyer because of his disorder.

Read more to find out.......

A few months back Kaju had called me

After examining him we had snacks and tea

He could not hear

From far or near

He said "Do something whatever it may be"

I sent him to an audiologist who was keen

That he wore a hearing aid which is not seen

For so it was

That was the cause

Of the smile on his face, which looked quite mean

He called me after a month and a half
I did not know whether to smile or laugh
He could hear me
And the humming of bee
And also when a cow was calling the calf

Though using a hearing aid, he had told none
Now listening to what others say, was just fun
He pretended he heard nothing
Though he could hear something
Of what was said about him, quite often

Earlier he had made his will in such a way
That everyone in his household could say
Just look after my health
For there is enough wealth
For one to enjoy without working a single day

After using the hearing aid the old man felt
That each one of them should tighten the belt
For being spendthrift
There would be a rift
About the property, if it is not properly dealt

Badam the eldest son had a great plan
He said " I'll mortgage the mansion if I can"
His wife agreed
"I think I need"
To go to Canary Islands to take a tan

The second son Akrot was a lazy lump
He felt that he was always in a sump
He wanted everything
And live like a king
Everyone else he wanted to dump

Son-in-law, Clove, led a luxurious life
He was enjoying this because of his wife
What he loved the most
Was eating the toast
After applying butter on it with a knife

The staff members too were waiting for a slice of the pie
It looked as if they were waiting for the old man to die
The old man was shocked
He decided he talked
To his lawyer to change the will, not tell him why

Sunday afternoon was time for family get together
Everyone would do something or the other
There was a huge hall
Where children with a ball
Would play games depending on the weather

By the side of the hall on the east
Was a room where family members would have their feast
Following that
They would chat
And listen to news or music at least

The second room was just by its side
The old man had got it modified
As a reading room
And no matter whom
He called for a chat, he would take them inside

Beside it was the third room in a row
It was meant for the servants though
While sipping tea
They would see
The movies which were popular, you know

The children were in the hall making noise
The staff was watching movies of their choice
When the new will was made
And the lawyer's bill was paid
The family members were listening to a melodious voice

The man who attempted robbery was God knows who
The time was between two-to-two to two- two
The old man raised an alarm
And also caught him by the arm
And he used skills of what he knew about Kung Fu

The robber panicked and began to run

He regretted that he forgot his gun

He tried to strangulate

The person at the gate

But could not as he was the tracheostomised one

The robber had managed to run away

It seems he was after the will that day

Who was the person

Who wanted this done

Was what the policeman could not say

The policeman of the case was a friend of mine
Together we would often chit chat and dine
I think I know it
Who is the culprit
He was pleased and said that it would be fine

I said one thing is quite clear

The person who ordered this is the one who could hear

When there was sound

All around

And that's the one person my dear

Explanation :

The person who ordered the thief to steal the will was Clove, Pista's spouse. He was the one who could hear when the meeting took place between the old man and the lawyer. As the children were making noise, the staff was watching movies and the family members were listening to music, when the new will was made. The only person who could hear during noisy surroundings was a person having Otosclerosis and that is Clove.

The old man made things all clear

Some of his assets were for his near and dear

But most of the property

He willed to a charity

For those children who could not hear

General Information

History

When a patient visits a doctor, the detailed history is essential and helpful in diagnosing the ailment. After name, address, age, occupation etc for identification; the main history starts with complaints specific to the ear, nose & throat. Then comes the general history like fever, headache, vomiting etc. Then comes the past history of major illnesses, operations etc. Then comes the personal history like history of smoking, drinking, hypertension, diabetes. Family history and previous treatment taken is also noted. It is best to write down all the complaints so that one does not forget. The complaints should be in chronological order. For example, pain in the left ear – 3 days, discharge from the left ear – 1 day....

Disorders are either congenital (since birth) or injury, infection, allergy, foreign bodies, neurological problems and tumors; either benign or malignant. All these maybe in the ear, nose and throat. However, loss of function are specific to the particular organ. For example, otosclerosis will give rise to deafness and tinnitus. Vertigo may sometimes be because of disorders of the ear. Facial palsy maybe due to otologic causes. Similarly, in the nose, there maybe nasal polyp, that is obstruction or breathing difficulty and bleeding from the nose. In the pharynx, there are problems of tonsils and adenoids. Submucous fibrosis is usually found in the Indian subcontinent, due to consumption of chewable tobacco (panmasala) and other irritants. Stomatitis maybe due to different causes. Difficulty in swallowing is maybe due to iron deficiency (anaemia).

Remember, ENT is a part of the whole body. Sometimes, ENT symptoms may be related to something happening somewhere else in the body. The most common being hyper-tension and diabetes. Diseases such as Kochs (Tuberculosis) will have ENT symptoms. These are psychosomatic disorders giving rise to ENT symptoms. So do not forget the role of mind and body when dealing with ENT disorder.

Do Not Use Ear Buds

As far as possible, do not use ear buds to clean the ear. Normally, there is wax in the ear which is meant for protection. It need not be removed. The ear contains migratory type of epithelium which means the ear is normally clean. If at all there is accumulated wax or dead skin, keratin, then the bud will push the matter further down in the canal. There have been cases when there's injury of the ear drum, when using the ear bud due to sudden movement of the head accidentally.

One may ask why nothing happens inspite of the fact that many people are using buds daily. My explanation is, as soon as we remove the wax, new wax is generated just as when we spit or swallow saliva, new saliva is formed in the oral cavity.

Diabetes Otitis Externa

Infection of the external ear is common and can be treated. But when it is associated with diabetes, it deserves a special mention because it becomes destructive. In diabetes pain is usually severe and unbearable and if not treated, there are complications.

If not treated, infection spread deeper and there maybe paralysis due to involvement of cranial nerves (facial).

Otitis Externa

In otitis externa, there is inflammation in the external ear due to water entering the ear or due to scratching. Otomycosis is fungal infection due to water entering the ear, prolonged use of antibiotic or steroid ear drops.

Some persons have a habit of scratching the ear using pins, keys etc. Fungal infection is common in monsoon, whether it rains or not. Hot and humid climate is ideal for fungal infection. Swimming is also a predisposing factor.

What not to do If there is an injury in the ear

Injury or slap on the ear or if there is a bomb explosion or crackers (blast injury) nearby then it is very important that no drops should be put in the ear. No water should be allowed to enter the ear. No oil should be put in the ear. In short, do not put anything in the ear

Otosclerosis or Otospongiosous

Otosclerosis or Otospongiosous is due to fixation of stapes to the oval window. There is conductive deafness in spite of normal drum and patent Eustachian tube. Such a person hears better in noisy surroundings (Paracusis Willisi). Tinnitus or noise in the ear may also be present. Patient has a choice of undergoing surgery or using the hearing aid.

Normally when a person talks in a quiet room one can hear the person properly. However, in a noisy environment, because of external noise, we don't hear clearly what the person is talking unless he talks louder than the surrounding noise. However, the person suffering from this disorder, does not hear the surrounding noise and its masking effect is not experienced. Hence the person hears clearly in a noisy environment.

How to talk to an elderly person

Some persons who are hard of hearing complain when talked too loudly and tell others not to shout. This appears paradoxical. But there's an explanation to this. In such persons, louder sounds are heard near their full intensity, although the threshold of hearing is raised.

In elderly people, there's loss of discrimination and hence it is difficult to differentiate similar sounding words. When talking to an elderly person it is better to go near, talk clearly and slowly. As far as possible, only one person should talk at one time. Avoid talking loudly from another room.

Use of hearing aids has helped many people hard of hearing. However, people should avoid use of hearing aids when there is loud sound around such as bomb or cracker explosions as loud noise is injurious to the inner ear. Continuous use of mobile phones, listening to loud music in excess will be harmful in the long run. Remember, moderation is the key.

Say "No To Smoking"

Everyone knows the bad effects of smoking. Apart from cancer, it is likely to affect hearing due to sensorineural hearing loss and the only cure is prevention. Hence say no to smoking (even passive).

In addition, tobacco in the form of chewing gives rise to gut mucous fibrosis (pre-malignant condition). Some people are more sensitive to the effect. They must avoid tobacco in any form like snuff or chewing.

Furuncle of the nose

If there is a boil on the nose, take care not to press it. Otherwise, there may be serious complications. If the person is diabetic, then it should be aggressively treated to prevent complication

Use of decongestant nasal drops

Avoid using nose drops/sprays containing decongestant. Immediately they open up the nose but they have a rebound phenomenon. They dry up the nose and the ciliary action is also impaired. After a time, one might be addicted and long-term use is not good.

What to do when there is bleeding from nose.

There are a few things one should know as to what should be done immediately before being attended by a physician. For example, if there is bleeding from the nose then the nose should be pressed for 4-5 minutes. Person should sit leaning the head forward. If the bleeding is from both the sides then the nose should be pressed on either side and keep the mouth open to breathe. If possible, ice pack or cold water mask may be applied to the nose. In adults, if there is hypertension, it should be brought under control.

STAPEDECTOMY

Short and simple is the surgery of Stapedectomy

Though how simple it is, you must not ask me

After premedication you take an incision

Placed endomeatal with great precision

Elevate the flap till there is a good exposure

Delicately removing the stapes superstructure

Elevate the mucosa over the oval window

Carefully measure the distance you must know

Then make a hole and put the piston

On putting the drum back, you complete the operation

May your successes make you not forget a failure

You see, the concerned person has lost his ear!

[* ***Stapedectomy :*** *This surgery is done in a patient suffering from otosclerosis*]

Nasal Allergy

A lovely young lady had nasal allergy
After taking some treatment she came to me
I asked what she was allergic to
She said if I knew that I'd not have come to you
I asked her when she gets all those sneezing
She said it is almost always in the evening
I asked her was it when her husband came home?
Yes, she said and there was no allergy when he went to Rome
I said this problem of yours is very very simple
As simple as that of hiding your pimple
You must avoid such things you are allergic to
She said instead of my husband I better avoid you!

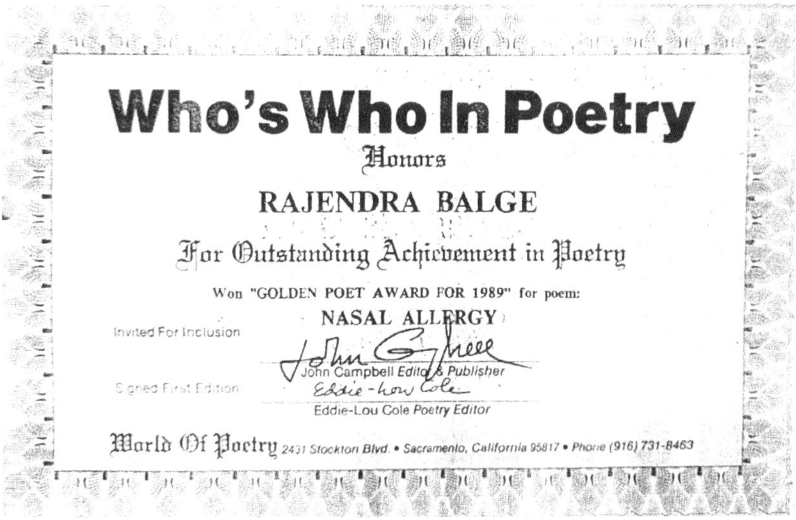
Who's Who In Poetry
Honors
RAJENDRA BALGE
For Outstanding Achievement in Poetry
Won "GOLDEN POET AWARD FOR 1989" for poem:
NASAL ALLERGY
Invited For Inclusion
John Campbell Editor & Publisher
Signed First Edition
Eddie-Lou Cole Poetry Editor
World Of Poetry 2431 Stockton Blvd. • Sacramento, California 95817 • Phone (916) 731-8463

Limerick on Vocal Nodule

There was a salesman who had hoarseness of voice
He used to shout and make a lot of noise
His nodule was removed
And his voice improved
Now he has started manufacturing toys.

Otolaryngologic Astrology

What your stars foretell about your ear, nose & throat disorders

Some stress that astrology is a science. They go to an extent to prove that it is a science and when the antagonists of astrology point out glaring errors in the forecasts the protagonists argue that no one can be perfect, even two ENT specialists will give two different diagnosis on the same patient. Does that mean that Otolaryngology is not a science?

Some say it is an Art, the art of cheating people. There is no science in it. How can you forecast anything? They claim. The Astrologers just cheat people, they say.

I say it is plain commerce. What do you think? No matter what you think I would bet my last paisa(if legally allowed) that everyone has an instinctive desire to know what is in store for him/her in future. Invariably one tries to find out what will happen. Some resort to astrology, some to palmistry, some to numerology etc.

If the forecast turns out to be correct they start believing in the particular method. If the forecast turns out to be wrong they say that is all humbug.

For reasons best known to them people read forecasts in newspapers, magazines, etc. and none worth its salt would avoid publishing forecasts. Some forecast people's future, some forecast in politics, some forecast economic issues etc

Now a days people have started using computers for forecasting. Anyone can forecast anything and some one at some time is likely to be correct. So be ready for your forecast.

In ENT diseases if something turns out to be correct it will be a mere coincidence.

Aries (March 20 - April 20)

Aries individuals are person of creative action/ They are usually in good health. They may get headaches off and on sometimes due to sinusitis. They may get burning in the throat perhaps due to hyperacidity. They have hardly any problem with their ears although in old age they will get presbyacusis.

Taurus (April 21 – May 21)

Taurians are possessive type of persons. They are usually in excellent health. They may get nasal allergy. As they love eating, over indulgence may give them stomatitis and may get itching in the ears which may be the first sign of diabetes mellitus.

Gemini (May 22 – June 21)

Gemini people are great thinkers. Their headaches are usually due to mental thinking. They may get trigeminal or glossopharyngeal neuralgia. They should also prevent cold blasts of air directly to the ears else they may land up with facial palsy.

Cancer (June 22 – July 22)

Cancer people are emotional people. They have a tendency to retain water which is likely to give Meniere's Syndrome. They may have hypertrophic rhinitis giving them nasal obstruction. In the throat, they may have cysts and may get mumps.

Leo (July 23 – Aug 22)

They are people of great determination. They may get tinnitus in the ears, or epistaxis. They may also get vocal cord palsy.

Virgo (Aug 23 – Sept 23)

They are painstaking people. They are likely to have sensorineural hearing loss, Vasomotor rhinitis and chronic granular pharyngitis.

Libra (Sept 24 – Oct 23)

They are born strategists. They are likely to have middle ear diseases, tonsillitis and adenoid problems. As they are cold and detached they are likely to have psychosomatic disorders in ENT

Scorpio (Oct 24 – Nov 23)

They are serious people. As they are sensitive, they are likely to have olitis externa, furuncle in the ears and nose and may get submucous fibrosis, if they have the habit of chewing betel nuts, tobacco etc.

Sagittarius (Nov 24- Dec 21)

Sagittarians are happy and cheerful. They may have injuries. During childhood they may put foreign bodies in their ears and nose. While brushing their teeth, they may injure their palate.

Capricorn (Dec 22 – Jan 20)

They are responsible people. They hold responsible positions. They may get otomycosis, chronic laryngitis and frontal sinusitis.

Aquarius (Jan 21 – Feb 19)

They are great humanitarians. They are likely to suffer from vasomotor rhinitis, neurodermatitis of the ear and P.V. Syndrome.

Pisces (Feb 20 – Mar 19)

They are people who are highly sympathetic. They should avoid drugs and alcohol. As they are likely to suffer from iatrogenic disorders like S. J. Syndrome, rhinitis medicamentosa and drug induced deafness.

Hoarseness of Voice

There was a pretty girl, and a pretty girl was she
She was quite upset when she came to me
I asked her what the problem was
She said to me after a brief pause
I have got hoarseness of voice
That was told me by many boys
So I went to a doctor who thought it was Ca
And advised me a scopy ofcourse under GA
So I turned to another who said its a cyst
While the third said its a polypi I insist
The fourth pronounced " આ તો vocal cord palsy છે"*
Don't do anything, you wont improve anyway
*The fifth exclaimed, "** આ છે Rinke's oedema"!!*
*"*** જો ના હોય તો concession આપીશ મારી ફી માં"*
So I have finally come to you, examine me please
I shall pay you handsomely, whatever your fees
A diagnosis of vocal nodules was made by me
I advised her MLS, vocal rest and speech therapy
She took my advice almost immediately
For she kept mum when I demanded my fee
However month later, she came for re-examination
She was subjectively better and there was no tension
Happily she gave me something very special
Don't get ideas, its nothing sensational

[This is vocal cord palsy]*
*[** This is Rinke's oedema]*
*[*** If it is not, I shall give concession in my fees]*

"What do we do to prevent spread of Infection and Allergy if the pathogen has reached your Ear, Nose or Throat"?

Written in March 2020

Normally, I do not give unsolicited advice. However, times are not normal. Hence, I am writing on how to prevent repeated infection and allergy. This might help even in viral infections, especially among vulnerable people.

REMEMBER -

1. A chain is as weak as a weakest link.
2. Reduce the number of Pathogens/Allergens (P/A)
3. Divert the path of P/A

1. **A chain is as weak as a weakest link:** Except in the patients who have undergone tracheostomy, the P/A reaches the lungs via the nose, nasopharynx, pharynx, larynx into the trachea or from the oral cavity to the pharynx, larynx into the trachea.

   P/A may enter indirectly from the eyes into the naso-lachrymal duct or through the ears into the eustachian tube though the chances of a virus taking this route is almost negligible. However, I am not sure whether it is absolutely

nil.
Normally, a patient having wax and intact tympanic membrane will not have any problem.

However, in patients who have perforations in the tympanic membrane and in patients who have undergone radical mastoidectomy, this possibility, though remote, exists.

Washing hands frequently is an excellent idea and so is putting on mask! However, it is not always possible to not touch the nose and inadvertently we may touch it or the mask may slip. So some P/A are likely to enter the nasal cavities and pharynx which remain the weakest link from where the P/A enters the lungs.

2. **Reduce the number of pathogens/allergens (P/A):**
a. Putting on mask - already advocated
b. Nose - nasal rinse. Blowing the nose clear
c. Oral cavity - gargles off and on
d. Posterior pharyngeal wall - gargles do not reach this site. So we have to drink fluids off and on and swallow saliva. Warm fluids are better.
e. Nasopharynx - this is the most difficult site to clear. Hence, I suggest applying nasal gel inside the nostrils and keep chewing something in the mouth and swallow the saliva. Ex: peppermint, cardamom, clove, raisins, liquorice etc. When we swallow saliva, the nasal secretions will pass through the nasopharynx into the oropharynx where it will mix with the oral secretions. The gel also helps to slow down the movement of P/A
3. **Divert the path of P/A:** Now the secretions from the nose, oral cavity and pharynx will be diverted to go into the

stomach where the Gastric Acid will eliminate them. And even if there is infection in the intestine, it can be managed better than infection in the lungs. For this, we have to swallow saliva off and on throughout the day.

Now a couple of things which should not be done.

a. Do not use decongestant nasal drops like oxymetazoline etc in the nose
b. Do not use earbuds

Compliance: For anything to be effective, compliance is required.

Chronology

- when we are taking a bath blow the nose and do nasal rinse
- Apply nasal gel
- When washing hands blow the nose clean and use saline nasal drops or spray.
- Drink fluids off and on and swallow saliva off and on
- After coming home when washing face, blow the nose clean.

In Poetry Form

A petite and vivacious girl asked me the other day
What would you do if the CORONA VIRUS comes in your way?
I said, first of all it cannot come in my way
As I would not go out but in my home, I will stay,
I would wash my hands and wear a mask,
As, if I do not wear it, I will be taken to task,
Now I'll tell you, what I would do if they enter the ears, nose or throat:
Yes, the chances of entering the throat via the ears is quite remote,
I will rinse my nose with warm salt water,
Making sure it is warm not hot or hotter,
I would keep myself clean, from head to toes,
I would apply some ghee or oil in the nose,
I would wash my hands, throughout the day,
I would blow my nose and use saline nasal spray,
I would gargle and keep my mouth clean,
I would drink warm fluids in between,
I would keep raisins, liquorice or cardamom in the mouth,
And keep swallowing saliva, there is no doubt.
I would not ask, what are others doing to prevent infection
I would ask, what I can do to make India a great nation.

How (?not) to write a letter? (!)

You should not write like this. This is a mirror-image letter. Hold this in front of a mirror and you will find it easy to read. I wrote such a letter to one of my school teachers. He would not take it lying down. He wrote a "cochlear" letter something like this :

www.ingramcontent.com/pod-product-compliance
Ingram Content Group UK Ltd.
Pitfield, Milton Keynes, MK11 3LW, UK
UKHW021409190726
13845UKWH00028B/971

9 789354 450082